Josie the Jewelry Fairy

Special thanks to Rachel Elliot

ISBN 978-0-545-70832-6

Previously published as Magical Crafts Fairies #4: *Josie the Jewellery-Making Fairy* by Orchard U.K. in 2014.

All rights reserved. Published by Scholastic Inc., 557 Broadway, New York, NY 10012, by arrangement with Rainbow Magic Limited.

12 11 10 9 8 7 6 5 4 3 2 1   15 16 17 18 19 20/0

Printed in the U.S.A.   40

This edition first printing, March 2015

Josie
the Jewelry
Fairy

by Daisy Meadows

SCHOLASTIC INC.

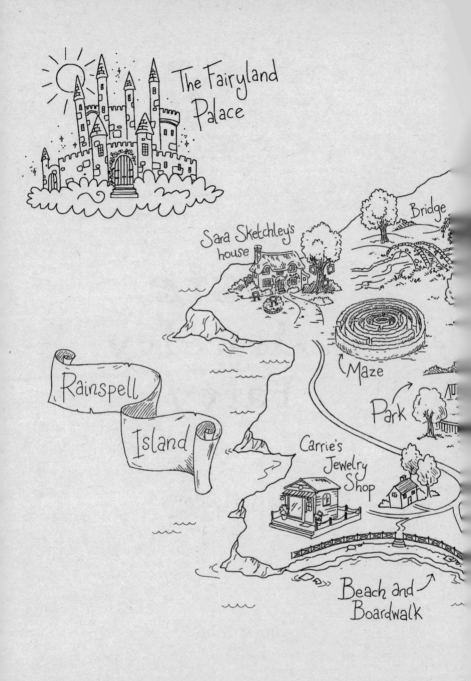

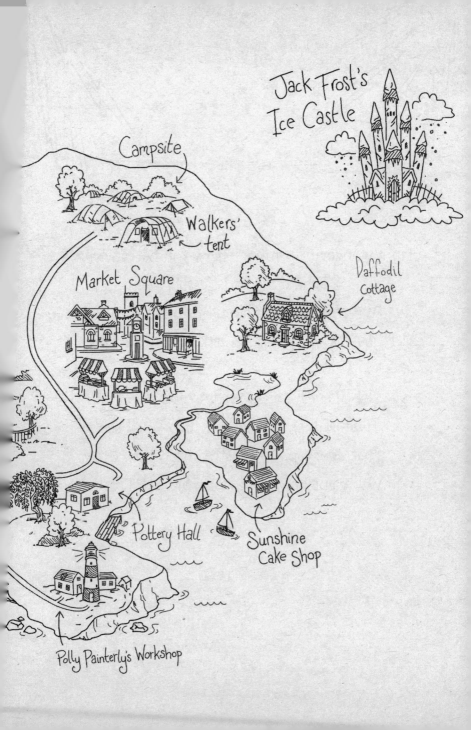

I'm a wonderful painter—have you heard of me?
Behold my artistic ability!
With palette, brush, and paints in hand,
I'll be the most famous artist in all the land!

The Magical Crafts Fairies can't stop me!
I'll steal their magic, and then you'll see
That everyone, no matter what the cost,
Will want a painting done by Jack Frost!

Contents

Golden Seashells

Rachel Walker sat up and yawned, then smiled as she remembered where she was. It was early in the morning, but the warm sun was already soaking through the canvas of her tent. She looked over at her best friend, Kirsty Tate, who was still curled up in her sleeping bag. So far, their vacation on Rainspell Island had been full of adventure!

"I wonder what today will bring," she whispered to herself.

Rachel leaned back on her pillow and thought about everything that had happened since they'd arrived. It was Crafts Week on the island, and so far the girls had tried pottery, drawing, and sewing. There were lots more crafts left to try, plus a competition and exhibition at the end of the week.

Things had gotten even more exciting when they met Kayla the Pottery Fairy, though. Rachel and Kirsty were secret friends with all the fairies. Now they were spending spring break together on their favorite island, *and* they were in the middle of a magical adventure!

Kirsty stirred in her sleep and rolled over. Rachel sat up and unzipped the tent flap. Sunlight spilled into the tent, turning everything golden. Kirsty yawned and opened her eyes.

"Good morning," she said, stretching her arms. "I was having a great dream. I think I sleep even better in the tent than I do in the bed and breakfast!"

Kirsty's family was staying at a little b and b in the village, and Rachel's family was camping. The girls had decided to spend every other night at each place all week, and it was turning out to be a lot of fun!

"I think I can hear Mom making breakfast," said Rachel, wriggling out of her sleeping bag. "Come on, I'm starving!"

The girls got dressed and pulled on their sandals.

"What crafts should we do today, Rachel?" asked Kirsty.

"Well, you know it's my mom's birthday,"

Rachel said. "I'd love to make something to give her later at the party."

Mr. Walker had organized a surprise party for his wife, and the girls could hardly wait. Just then, there was a tap on the tent flap.

"Come in!" said Rachel and Kirsty together.

Mr. Walker came into the tent and put a finger to his lips. He looked very excited.

"I just want to show you the present I got for your mom," he whispered to Rachel. "I had them handmade by Carrie Silver, who runs the jewelry shop down by the water."

He held out a tiny velvet box. Rachel
took it and opened the lid.
Sitting on a bed of ivory silk
was a pair of gold earrings,
shaped like seashells.

"They're beautiful,"
she said in a soft
voice.

"Really pretty,"
Kirsty agreed.

Rachel picked up one
of the earrings—but then something
awful happened. The seashell fell off of
the rest of the earring. It was broken!

"I'm sorry!" cried Rachel, feeling
guilty. "I was trying so hard to be
careful!"

"It wasn't your fault," said Mr. Walker,
examining the earrings. "Look—they're

both broken. It must have happened while the box was in my pocket."

He looked sad, and Rachel gave him a big hug.

"Don't worry, Dad," she said. "I have an idea. Carrie Silver is running a jewelry-making class in her shop. We

could go down there and make
something for Mom's birthday ourselves."

"That's a great idea," Kirsty chimed
in, giving Mr. Walker a reassuring smile.
"We can take the earrings back to be
fixed at the same time."

Mr. Walker agreed. Just then, they
heard Mrs. Walker's voice.

"Breakfast's ready," she called. "Come
and get it, everyone!"

They hurried out of the tent and filled
their plates with bacon, eggs, potatoes,
and fruit. The girls wished Mrs. Walker
a happy birthday and ate their breakfast
as fast as they could.

"What's the rush?" asked Mrs. Walker
with a laugh.

"We're just excited to get to the craft
workshop in town," said Rachel with a

grin. "Come on, Kirsty, let's go!"

The girls waved good-bye and hurried off before Mrs. Walker could ask what sort of crafts they were going to be doing. They didn't want her to guess that they were making jewelry for her birthday!

Scattered Pearls

The girls ran through the buttercup-filled fields toward the village. The sparkling blue sea stretched out in front of them. A light breeze lifted spray from the tips of the waves.

"Wouldn't it be wonderful to live here year-round?" said Kirsty as they reached the village.

"Maybe," said Rachel. "But I love coming here for vacation—it makes it extra-special when we only have a few days on the island."

The girls linked arms when they reached Main Street. There were already lots of people strolling in and out of the gift shops and taking photos of the quaint little buildings. Kirsty stopped next to a pretty souvenir shop with flags hanging in the window.

"Look, this store sells jewelry," she said. "Maybe we could get some ideas to inspire us."

The girls looked over the jewelry display, but they weren't very impressed.

"That necklace is broken," said Rachel, pointing to a chipped pendant on a silver chain. "And all the bracelets are facing the wrong way, so we can't even see them."

"Let's try the next store," Kirsty suggested.

But the next store's jewelry display was even more disappointing. There were a lot of broken pins, and the gold watches looked dull and unpolished. In fact, in every store the girls tried, all the jewelry was ruined!

"The strange thing is that all the other souvenirs in those stores look so clean and new," said Rachel.

Kirsty glanced into the nearest store window. Aside from a jar of tarnished silver rings, the window display was bright and colorful. There were lots of  wooden toys, hand-painted plates, and shiny ornaments.

"Yes, that *is* weird," she said, sounding

14

thoughtful. "Rachel, do you think that Jack Frost and his goblins have something to do with this?"

"I'm sure they do," said Rachel. "I bet the stores here wouldn't usually have broken jewelry on display."

On their first day on Rainspell Island, Kayla the Pottery Fairy had fluttered out of a clay pot and whisked them off to Fairyland. She brought them to the grand opening of the fairies' Crafts Week! The Magical Crafts Fairies had shown Kirsty and Rachel their special objects, which ensured that arts and crafts were fun for everyone. But after King Oberon and Queen Titania announced that they would choose the best crafts to decorate their Fairyland Palace, everything went all wrong.

Jack Frost and his goblins had thrown paint-filled balloons into the crowd, splattering everyone with bright green paint! Then they snatched the magic objects from the Magical Crafts Fairies and disappeared to the human world. Jack Frost thought that he was the greatest artist ever. He had stolen the objects so that no one could ever be better than him.

"So far, we've helped Kayla the Pottery Fairy, Annabelle the Drawing Fairy, and Zadie the Sewing Fairy get their magic objects back," said Kirsty, thinking back over the last few days.

"But there are still four more objects to find," said Rachel. "We have to keep looking, or arts and crafts will be a disaster forever!"

"Yes," said Kirsty with a groan, "here *and* in Fairyland."

At the end of the village's Main Street, the road widened and led down to the ocean. As the girls stepped onto the boardwalk, they saw a woman on her hands and knees. It was Artemis Johnson, the organizer of Crafts Week. She looked very upset!

"Artie, are you hurt?" called Rachel, hurrying over to her.

"No, I'm fine," said Artie. "But my pearl necklace just broke, and the pearls rolled all over the boardwalk! How will I ever find them all?"

17

Jinxed Jewelry

"We'll help!" said the girls right away.

A moment later, all three of them were crawling around the boardwalk on their hands and knees. The pearls had rolled into all different cracks and crevices, but Rachel and Kirsty found them all.

"Wow, you must have amazing eyesight," said Artie gratefully as Rachel handed her the last pearl.

The girls exchanged secret smiles. After all, they were used to spotting tiny fairies!

Artie carefully put the pearls in her bag, along with the broken string. "I'll ask Carrie Silver to fix it for me," she said. "She's a wonderful jeweler."

"We're on our way to her shop now," said Kirsty. "Should we all go together?"

"That sounds great," said Artie.

They walked along the boardwalk together, enjoying the soft summer breeze.

"Are you having fun on Rainspell?" asked Artie.

"We love it here," said Rachel with a big smile. "Actually, this is where we first met and became friends."

Artie was about to reply when a burst of noise from the beach interrupted her. Some boys in big green sun hats were messing around at the edge of the water, trying to push one another in. They were shouting and laughing loudly.

"What a commotion," said Artie with a frown. "Why are they making so much noise?"

"They must have already been to the jewelry workshop," said Kirsty, looking closely. "They're wearing every kind of jewelry I can think of!"

The boys all had beaded necklaces

dangling around their necks. They were wearing so many bracelets that you could hardly see their arms, and there were even beaded charms dangling from their sun hats!

After a few minutes, the boys stopped pushing one another around. They started picking up shells from the beach and putting them into a bucket, instead.

"Oh, no! Collecting seashells isn't allowed on Rainspell Island anymore," said Artie, peering across the sand at the boys. "We're trying really hard to preserve the natural seashore."

"Maybe we should go and tell them that," Rachel suggested.

But they had only taken a few steps toward the boys when they heard a loud, angry squawk from above. A large seagull flew directly at the group of boys!

"Run!" yelled the boys.

They sprinted down the beach, shouting the whole way. The seagull circled above them a few times, and then flew back inland. The girls shrugged.

"Carrie's jewelry shop is right up there," said Artie.

She pointed to a little wooden store overlooking the beach. It was painted sky blue, and the window that faced the ocean stretched from the floor all the way up to the ceiling.

"Carrie sits in that window to design her jewelry," Artie told the girls. "The seashore inspires all of her designs."

As Rachel, Kirsty, and Artie reached the shop, two girls walked out, shaking their heads.

"I give up on jewelry-making," said the dark-haired girl.

"Me, too," said the redhead. "I'm just not good enough."

Rachel and Kirsty exchanged a worried look. Inside, the jewelry-making workshop didn't seem to be going very well. Beads were rolling all over the floor, and strings were breaking. Carrie was dashing from person to person, trying to help fix each problem, but things kept going wrong all around her!

"Carrie, what's going on here?" exclaimed Artie.

Carrie stopped rushing around for a moment and gave Artie a hug. Then she ran her fingers through her short silver hair, making it stand up on end.

"It's a total disaster," she said. "Everything is going wrong today. I don't know what to do!"

"I'm so sorry to hear that," said Artie. "I came to ask you to fix a necklace and to bring you two extra students for your workshop. But maybe I should come back tomorrow."

"No, please don't go!" said Carrie, giving the girls a warm, welcoming smile. "First, let me see this broken necklace."

Artie handed Carrie the necklace, and she immediately cut off a piece of string from a roll on the table.

"This is a five-minute job," she said, patting Artie's arm. "No problem."

But as she spoke, the pearls dropped off

the end of the string and rolled away again. Carrie groaned and started to kneel down, but Rachel stopped her.

"We'll get them," she said with a smile.

It only took Rachel and Kirsty a few seconds to gather the pearls.

"Thank you, girls," said Carrie, putting the pearls into a little pot. "I'm so clumsy today! Would you like to look around and see what you might want to make? I'll come help you as soon as I fix Artie's necklace."

"Are you sure you're not too busy?" asked Kirsty.

Things were still going wrong in the jewelry workshop all around them. Students holding bits of broken wire and snapped string were waiting to talk to Carrie.

"I would love for you to join the workshop," said Carrie with a smile. "It hasn't been a *total* disaster today—I had a group of boys here earlier who made some really amazing beaded jewelry."

Rachel glanced at Kirsty. It was good to hear that some people had managed to make nice jewelry! Maybe Carrie's problems had nothing to do with Jack Frost, after all.

"The boys wanted to make jewelry out

of seashells," Carrie went on. "They got annoyed when I told them about preserving the natural seashore, and they stormed off."

"I bet those were the boys we saw on the beach," said Artie.

She started to tell Carrie about the boys, and the girls wandered off to look around the little shop. It was full of delicate jewelry, all inspired by the ocean and the shore. Rachel picked up a silver pin shaped like a starfish.

"I might make a pin like this," she said. "Isn't it pretty, Kirsty?"

But Kirsty didn't reply. Rachel looked around in surprise, and saw her gazing at a wooden jewelry box on a shelf in the corner. The box was glowing with a faint light, and there was a beautiful painting of a fairy on the front.

"Rachel, look at the picture!" whispered Kirsty, excited. "Should we open it?"

"Of course!" said Rachel.

Together, the girls lifted the lid of the jewelry box — and out fluttered Josie the Jewelry Fairy!

Footprints in the Sand

Josie was wearing a sparkly yellow skirt with a wide belt, and a cropped peach top. Beautiful beads dangled around her neck, and pretty bracelets jangled on her wrists. She held out her hands to the girls.

"Rachel and Kirsty, I need your help!" she gasped. "I have to find my magic beaded ribbon. Jewelry is a mess—in the human world, and in Fairyland, too!"

"Of course we'll help you," said Kirsty. "What does your magic ribbon look like?"

"It's pink, and it has three sparkly beads on it," said Josie, tucking her chocolate-brown hair behind her ears. "Until I find it and take it back to Fairyland, no one anywhere will be able to make jewelry!"

Suddenly, Rachel had a thought.

"Carrie said that the boys who were in the shop earlier made some wonderful jewelry," she said. "How could they have done that?"

"They must have had my magic

34

ribbon!" Josie exclaimed, clapping her tiny hands. "I knew you would be able to help me! Where are the boys now?"

"When we last saw them, they were on the beach," said Kirsty. "If we hurry, we might be able to catch up with them."

"Good idea," said Rachel. "Before we go, just let me give Carrie the earrings my dad needs to have fixed."

Josie hid under the brim of Rachel's sun hat, and the girls hurried over to Carrie, who was still trying to fix Artie's necklace. Rachel pulled the little velvet box out of her pocket and showed Carrie the golden seashell earrings.

"I'll take a look at them as soon as I'm done fixing Artie's necklace," Carrie promised.

"We just have to run out for a minute," Kirsty added. "But we'll be back soon!"

Carrie was too busy to ask where they were going. The girls hurried onto the beach and looked around, but the boys were nowhere to be seen.

"It'll be easier to search if we're all fairies," said Josie. "Find a place to hide, and I'll use my magic!"

The girls noticed a little row of colorful

beach umbrellas nearby. One was open,
so they darted behind it.

Josie fluttered out from under Rachel's
sun hat and waved her wand. For a
moment, all the girls could see was
sparkling dust. Then they were fluttering
in midair next to Josie!

"Come on," said Rachel. "Let's find
those boys!"

The three fairies flew out from behind the umbrella and over the beach. Right away, Kirsty spotted lots of big footprints in the sand.

"Those almost look like goblin footprints!" said Rachel.

The fairies followed the trail until they found the group of boys. They were still wearing their green sun hats and beaded jewelry, but now they were building sandcastles. From above, the fairies could see something amazing—the boys had green feet!

"The *boys* are making the footprints," said Josie. "How is that possible?"

"Those aren't boys," said Rachel. "They're goblins!"

At that moment, one of the goblins started shouting and waving his arms. Then he pushed the goblin next to him, who fell over and squished a sandcastle. Soon, all the goblins were arguing, pushing one another, and kicking the sandcastles.

"Let's fly down," said Kirsty. "They're arguing too much to notice us!"

The three fairies hid behind the tower of a nearby sandcastle. A goblin with a splotchy face picked up a red plastic shovel and started digging. Then another goblin elbowed him in the ribs and snatched the shovel.

"My turn!" he squawked.

He started digging, too, but soon a third goblin grabbed the shovel from him!

"Why do they only have one shovel?" asked Rachel. "And what are they digging for? They're not picking up shells anymore."

"Maybe they think they'll find buried treasure," said Kirsty with a wink.

Suddenly there was a loud squawk, and a seagull landed next to them on the sandcastle.

"Hello!" said Rachel with a smile. "Kirsty, this is the same seagull we saw earlier—the one who scared the goblins away."

The seagull squawked again, and Josie smiled. The girls remembered that all fairies could speak to animals.

"He says hello," Josie told them.
"Seagull, do you know what the goblins
are doing here on the beach?"

The seagull gave a few more squawks,
and Josie turned to the girls.

"He thinks that the goblins have lost
something," she said. "They've been
looking for a long time."

Just then, some
beaded charms
dropped off one
goblin's sun hat.
Another goblin's
necklace
snapped, and the
beads scattered
across the sand.

"That's strange,"

said Rachel. "They have Josie's ribbon, so their jewelry shouldn't break."

"Oh!" exclaimed Kirsty, her eyes wide. "Maybe that's what they've lost—Josie's magic ribbon!"

Green
Ice Cream

Hearts thumping with excitement, the three friends fluttered into the air and spread out.

"Fly low over the beach and look carefully," said Josie. "We have to find my magic ribbon before the goblins do!"

Rachel saw a flash in the sunlight and zoomed toward it, but it was just a shiny pebble. Kirsty gasped when she saw

something sparkling down by the water.
But when she flew closer, she realized
that it was just a piece of wet seaweed.
Josie hovered near the goblins, in case
they found the charm. She edged closer
to try to see into the hole they were
digging—and then one of the goblins
gave an angry screech.

"A fairy!" he yelled. "There's a fairy
spying on us!"

He kicked sand at Josie, and
some of it went in her eyes.

Unable to see, she zigzagged through the
air, trying to get away. Rachel and
Kirsty zoomed to her side and pulled her
to safety behind a plastic bucket.

"More fairies!" the goblins squawked.
"Get them!"

But then the fairies heard one of the
goblins yelp. The next thing they knew,
the group of goblins was running away
down the beach.

"Why did they leave?" asked Kirsty.
"What did they see?"

While Josie wiped the sand out of her eyes, Kirsty and Rachel peeked around the side of the bucket. In the distance, close to the edge of the water, they could see a glow. It was obviously something magic!

"That's my ribbon, I'm sure of it!" said Josie over their shoulders.

"But the goblins have a big head start," Kirsty said with a groan. "We'll never catch up to them."

"Then we just have to outsmart them," said Rachel. "Quick, Josie—can you turn us back into humans and disguise us as ice-cream sellers? If there's one thing we know about goblins, it's that they're very, very greedy!"

The only thing on the beach was a striped awning, so the three fairies hid behind it. Josie waved her wand, and instantly, the girls were human-sized again! They were wearing white jackets and little white hats. Each of them held a tray of green ice-cream cups. They walked out from behind the awning, and Josie used her magic to play the sort of tinkly music that ice-cream trucks use.

"Free ice cream!" called Rachel at the top of her lungs. "Get your free ice cream here!"

The goblins stopped in their tracks and turned around. The splotchy one was already drooling.

"We can get the ribbon in a minute," the girls heard one of them say. "There's time to grab some ice cream."

They all ran up to Rachel and Kirsty, stumbling over their own feet and pushing one another out of the way.

"Give us our free ice cream *now*!" they shouted.

While Rachel and Kirsty handed out the ice cream, Josie flew down to get her magic ribbon. But just then, the splotchy goblin turned around and saw her flying toward the ribbon.

"STOP!" he shouted.

He kicked wildly, and his enormous foot scooped up a ton of sand. It hit Josie and knocked her sideways! Another

goblin sprinted over to the ribbon and grabbed it.

"Got it!" he squawked, holding it above his head like a trophy. "Ha ha, little fairy, you're too slow!"

The goblins cheered and snickered, their faces now covered in green ice cream. Josie flew back to the girls, wings drooping.

"I'm never going to get my ribbon back now," she said sadly.

Kirsty looked up and saw the seagull circling high overhead.

"Maybe we could ask the nice seagull for help," she said.

"I have one cup of ice cream left," said Rachel. "I wonder if he'd like some."

They waved at the seagull and he landed beside them. Rachel offered him the ice cream. While he ate it, Josie explained what had happened.

"Will you help me get my magic ribbon back?" she asked hopefully.

The girls couldn't understand the

seagull's reply, but he nodded his head and Josie smiled.

"He says yes," she said. "The goblins have been messing up the beach, so he wants them to go home, too."

The goblins were skipping down the beach, tossing the ribbon between them.

SQUAWWWWK!

The seagull swooped at the goblins, flying so low that he could have pecked their ears. The goblins cowered and squealed.

"Get away!" they wailed. "Leave us alone!"

The seagull squawked again. He was so loud that the goblins clapped their hands over their big ears and ran.

"Look!" cried Rachel, pointing and jumping up and down.

In their fright, the goblins had dropped the magic ribbon!

Sparkly Surprises

The seagull grabbed the magic ribbon in his beak and flew back to Josie. The beads on the ribbon twinkled as he handed it to her. It immediately shrank to fairy-size.

"Thank you!" said Josie, glowing. "Now I can fix everything!"

With a wave of Josie's wand, the shells from the goblins' bucket were returned to the beach where they belonged. Rachel's and Kirsty's disguises disappeared, too—they were back in their normal clothes and sun hats again.

"You've all been so wonderful," said Josie, smiling at Rachel, Kirsty, and the seagull. "Thank you for everything you've done. Jewelry is safe again because of you!"

"We were happy to help," said Kirsty.

Rachel nodded, and the seagull squawked in agreement.

"I hope we'll meet again one day," said Josie.

She waved good-bye and disappeared in a twinkling flash. The seagull hopped away across the sand, and Rachel and Kirsty smiled at each other.

"That's another one of the Magical Crafts Fairies' objects that Jack Frost can't use," said Rachel. "Now there are only three more to find!"

"But first we have to make our presents for your mom," Kirsty reminded her. "Come on!"

They ran back to the jewelry store. This time, it seemed like a very different place. There was a lot of laughter and a

buzz of excitement in the workshop.
Carrie was walking slowly around the
tables, checking to make sure that
everyone was doing OK. She smiled as
the girls sat at an empty table, and came
over to see them.

"Things have really calmed down
here," she said. "It was a bit of a crazy
morning, but now the jewelry-making is
going very well. I even had time to fix
your mom's earrings."

She handed Rachel the little velvet box.
Inside, the golden seashell earrings were
perfect again.

"Thank you so much," said Rachel.
"Mom will love them!"

Artie joined them and showed the girls
that she was wearing her pearl necklace.

"Carrie fixed it perfectly," she said.

"She's like a magic fairy, fixing all the jewelry so fast!"

The girls exchanged a secret smile. Little did Artie know that magic really *was* involved in jewelry-making!

"The trays in front of you have all sorts of beads, wires, threads, and clasps

for your jewelry," Carrie told the girls. "You can make whatever you want, and I'll help you if you get stuck. Have fun!"

Looking through the little trays, Rachel found some beautiful wooden beads. Each one had a different type of seashell painted on it.

"I think I'll make Mom a necklace with these beads," she said.

"I'll make a bracelet to match," said Kirsty, excited. "Then she'll have a whole matching set, because the earrings are seashells, too!"

The girls put their heads down and got to work.

That evening, the girls took Mrs. Walker for a walk along the cliffs while her surprise party was being set up. When they came back to the campsite,

Mrs. Walker's mouth fell open. Strings of twinkly lights were draped from tent to tent. Mr. Walker and Mr. and Mrs. Tate were standing around a glowing campfire, and there was a little pile of presents on a nearby table. There was even a big HAPPY BIRTHDAY banner! Mrs. Tate had baked a cake, and Mr. Tate was busy toasting marshmallows. Mrs. Walker couldn't believe her eyes.

"Happy birthday!" shouted the girls.

Everyone laughed and hugged Mrs. Walker, who was too surprised to speak. She blew out the candles on her cake and then sat down to open her presents.

"What beautiful earrings!" she cried, putting them on right away. "And a necklace and bracelet to match? I've never had such pretty jewelry!"

The girls told her all about making the necklace and the bracelet. Then Mrs. Tate asked to see the earrings, and Kirsty and Rachel slipped away to eat their toasted marshmallows.

"I have an extra surprise for you," said Rachel. "While we were in the shop, I made you something."

She gave Kirsty a little friendship bracelet in blue, pink, and lilac. Kirsty hugged her and laughed.

"I have a surprise for you, too," she said—pulling out a red, gold, and orange friendship bracelet!

"I guess that shows that we were made to be best friends!" Rachel giggled.

They tied the bracelets around each other's wrists. Then Kirsty gasped. On each of the friendship bracelets, a tiny, sparkling bead had appeared.

"They must be a thank-you gift from Josie," said Rachel. "What a wonderful way to end a surprise-filled day!"

RAINBOW magic™

THE MAGICAL CRAFTS FAIRIES

Rachel and Kirsty have found Kayla,
Annabelle, Zadie, and Josie's missing magic
objects. Now it's time for them to help

Violet
the Painting Fairy!

Join their next adventure
in this special sneak peek. . . .

Paint Problems

"We're not far from the lighthouse now, Kirsty," said Rachel Walker. The best friends were walking along the cliff toward the Rainspell Island Lighthouse. "Dad said we can't miss it! I wonder what he meant?"

"We'll find out soon!" Kirsty Tate replied. "I'm so glad we came to

Rainspell for another vacation, Rachel. There's no other place like it in the whole world!"

The girls were spending their spring break on Rainspell Island. They were taking turns staying with Kirsty's mom and dad at their bed and breakfast one night, and then with Rachel's parents at the campsite the next night.

"Plus, it's an extra-special vacation because it's Rainspell Crafts Week," Rachel pointed out. "*And* because of our adventures with the Magical Crafts Fairies!"

When the girls arrived on Rainspell Island a few days earlier, Kayla the Pottery Fairy had invited them to Fairyland, where a Crafts Week was also taking place. Kayla and the other

Magical Crafts Fairies were organizing the event. Kayla told the girls that King Oberon and Queen Titania would choose the most beautiful crafts, and use them to decorate their royal palace.

But as the queen welcomed everyone to Crafts Week, Jack Frost and his goblins had hurled paint-filled balloons into the crowd! The Magical Crafts Fairies and even Queen Titania herself had been splattered with bright green paint. In all the chaos and confusion, Jack Frost and his goblins had stolen the Magical Crafts Fairies' special objects. They were the source of the fairies' powerful magic!

Jack Frost had declared that he was the best artist ever, and he'd taken the magic objects to ensure that no one else could ever outdo him. As everyone watched helplessly, Jack Frost had magically whisked himself and the goblins away, to hide the objects in the human world. The fairies had been horribly upset, but Rachel and Kirsty stepped forward right away to offer their help. The girls were determined to prevent crafts everywhere from turning into complete disasters!

"Thank goodness we already found Kayla's vase, Annabelle's pencil sharpener, Zadie's thimble, and Josie's ribbon," Kirsty said. "I really enjoyed our pottery, drawing, sewing, and jewelry-making workshops."

"Me, too," Rachel agreed. "But they would have been totally ruined if the fairies hadn't gotten their magic objects back just in time!"

Kirsty nodded. "I can't wait to try

Polly Painterly's class at the lighthouse today," she said eagerly. "Painting is one of my favorite things!"

"But what do you think the class will be like, now that Violet the Painting Fairy's magic paintbrush is missing?" Rachel asked anxiously.

"Well, as Queen Titania always says, we have to wait for the magic to come to us and see!" Kirsty reminded her.

RAINBOW magic ™

Which Magical Fairies Have You Met?

- ❏ The Rainbow Fairies
- ❏ The Weather Fairies
- ❏ The Jewel Fairies
- ❏ The Pet Fairies
- ❏ The Dance Fairies
- ❏ The Music Fairies
- ❏ The Sports Fairies
- ❏ The Party Fairies
- ❏ The Ocean Fairies
- ❏ The Night Fairies
- ❏ The Magical Animal Fairies
- ❏ The Princess Fairies
- ❏ The Superstar Fairies
- ❏ The Fashion Fairies
- ❏ The Sugar & Spice Fairies
- ❏ The Earth Fairies

SCHOLASTIC

Find all of your favorite fairy friends at
scholastic.com/rainbowmagic

HiT entertainment

RMFAIRY10